# I LIKE YOUR BUTTONS!

WRITTEN BY *Sarah Marwil Lamstein*

ILLUSTRATED BY *Nancy Cote*

Albert Whitman & Company

Morton Grove, Illinois

Library of Congress Cataloging-in-Publication Data

Lamstein, Sarah Marwil, 1943-
I like your buttons! / by Sarah Marwil Lamstein; illustrated by Nancy Cote.
p.  cm.
Summary: When a little girl compliments her teacher about the buttons
on her outfit, it starts a chain reaction of goodwill, good deeds,
and thoughtfulness throughout the day.
ISBN 0-8075-3510-9
[1. Kindness—Fiction.  2. Thoughtfulness—Fiction.]  I. Cote, Nancy, ill.  II. Title.
PZ7.L215Iae 1999
[E]—DC21  98-29561
CIP
AC

Text copyright © 1999 by Sarah Marwil Lamstein.
Illustrations copyright © 1999 by Nancy Cote.
Published in 1999 by Albert Whitman & Company,
6340 Oakton Street, Morton Grove, Illinois 60053-2723.
Published simultaneously in Canada by General Publishing, Limited, Toronto.
Printed in the United States of America.
10 9 8 7 6 5 4 3 2 1

The paintings were done in acrylics, gouache, and watercolor pencil.
The text typeface is AG Book Rounded.
The design is by Scott Piehl.

To my dear ones — Josh, Emily, and Abby
S. M. L.

To Irene, Mark, and Luke,
who always have nice things to say
N. C.

Appreciative thanks to my editor, Abby Levine,
for her wisdom and her encouragement
S. M. L.

ne day, Cassandra's teacher, Ms. Sutton-Jones, wore a blouse with big, glittery buttons.

"I like your buttons, Ms. Sutton-Jones," Cassandra said.

"Why, thank you, dear. You've made my day!"

Ms. Sutton-Jones spied Ms. Avery, the custodian, pushing her broom through the hall.

"These floors shine like the inside of a palace!" called Ms. Sutton-Jones.

Ms. Avery looked up and smiled. Still smiling, she pushed her broom toward Mr. Diaz's second grade.

Mr. Diaz was peering out the door.
"Your kids are the tidiest!" Ms. Avery exclaimed.
Mr. Diaz chuckled.

He turned to his class and sang out "Snack time!" before the second grade had finished spelling.

Sharon was so tickled to have snack time in the middle of spelling that she shared her chips with Rhonda. Mr. Diaz always said sharing was wonderful.

"Mmmmm-boy!" said Rhonda as she munched her chips. "My favorites!"

At recess, Rhonda kicked the ball so hard her shoe flew off, and her team won the game.

Philip was so proud to be on the winning team ...

that after school he taught his brother Sam
"The Itsy-Bitsy Spider."

Sam practiced the song with his fingers until his mama got home from work. "Look what Philip showed me!" Sam shouted.

Mama sat right down and took both Sam and Philip on her lap.

When Papa walked in the door, they were laughing and snuggling. Papa laughed too, even louder.

"I'll go get dinner!" Papa said, and he ran all the way to Al's Bar-B-Q.

"Slather on the hot sauce, Al," he said. "You make the best ribs in the neighborhood."

Al puffed out his chest and slathered on the hot sauce. Then he called to his helper, "Take a few minutes off, Julian. You deserve it."

Julian sat on the back stoop and sipped a
lemonade, happy to be out of the hot kitchen.
    "Here, kitty," he said to the cat who lived in back
of the restaurant. "Want some ribs?" He held out
a string of beef.

After work, the cat rubbed against his leg.

"Why not?" said Julian, and he scooped him up.

"I'm bringing him home, Al," he called.

"Why not?" Al said.

In the morning, Julian's daughter awoke and found a cat resting on her bed. He was purring softly.

"Daddy!" she called.

Julian came into her room. "You like him, princess?" he asked.

The cat opened his eyes.
"His eyes are so big and bright!" Cassandra said.
"I think I'll call him Buttons."